TEDD ARNOLD

HUGGLY™
GETS DRESSED

SCHOLASTIC INC.

Cartwheel
·B·O·O·K·S·®

New York Toronto London Auckland Sydney Mexico City New Delhi Hong Kong

Look for Huggly in Scholastic's  **CD-ROM**

Library of Congress Cataloging-in-Publication Data
Arnold, Tedd.
    Huggly gets dressed / by Tedd Arnold.
      p. cm. — (Monsters under the bed)
    "Cartwheel books."
    Summary: A monster from under the bed tries to wear people clothes.
    ISBN 0-439-10268-5
    [1. Monsters — Fiction.   2. Clothing and dress — Fiction.]
  I. Title. II. Series.
  PZ7.A7379Hu 1997
  [E] — dc21

97-18777
CIP
AC

10 9 8 7 6 5 4 3 2 1

9/9 0/0 01 02 03 04

Printed in the U.S.A. 24
First printing, September 1999

Huggly peeked out from under the bed.

It was dark and quiet in the room. And messy. Perfect! He didn't want to wake the people child on the bed.

He hopped across the room on tippy-toes.
On tippy-top. On tippy-tail.

He bumped his head.

Things fell onto the floor. It was the stuff people wear on their bodies.

He wondered why they wear the stuff.
He wondered how.
Huggly decided to try for himself.

A bright red-and-yellow striped thing had a nice hole for his tail.

He slipped his arms into a blue thing.

He found a pair of orange things for his toes.

He pulled long purple things over his hands.

A white thing fit snugly on his head.

There was a green thing that he just couldn't figure out.

Huggly said to himself, "So this is how people dress!" There was a knock on the door. "Time to wake up, Sleepyhead," the people mother said. "Do you need help getting dressed?"

Huggly froze with fear. What if the people caught him? "Oh no!" he said out loud before he could stop himself.

"Did you say no?" the mother asked. "Are you sure?"
She turned the knob to open the door.

Huggly had to act quickly. Pulling things off his arms and legs, he turned and ran...

bump...right into Sleepyhead.

ust as the door swung open, Huggly dived under the bed.

"Silly, Sleepyhead." The mother laughed.
"How did you get dressed like that?"

"A...a...monster under the bed...," Sleepyhead mumbled
"That goofy monster again?" his mother said.
"Tell me all about it."